Let's Go to the
HARDWARE STORE

ANNE ROCKWELL
illustrated by MELISSA IWAI

Christy Ottaviano Books

HENRY HOLT AND COMPANY

NEW YORK

When we moved into
our bigger house,
everything needed fixing.
That's what Mommy said.

Daddy said
he could fix it all
if he had some
new tools.

"Don't forget the picture hangers,"
Mommy said as we left.
Then off we went to the hardware store,
Daddy and Flora and me.

Daddy saw a brand-new hammer
that would come in handy
and was better than his old one.
We put that handy new hammer in the cart.

TYPES *of* HAMMERS

FRAMING   TACK   SLEDGE   BALL-PEEN   MALLET   CLAW

So many screwdrivers—
we couldn't decide which one to get.
Flora liked the one with a yellow handle.
I liked the red one best.

Daddy chose a whole set of screwdrivers.

TYPES *of* SCREWDRIVERS

PHILLIPS HEAD   FLAT HEAD

We had to get spackle and a putty knife
to fix the crack in the ceiling.
Sandpaper would smooth the spackle
when it was dry.

We got a can of paint and a brush
with shiny black bristles.

SPACKLE

PUTTY
KNIFE

SANDPAPER

PAINT

PAINTBRUSH

The crack was too high for Daddy to reach,
so he needed a stepladder.
We chose the bright yellow one.

Daddy got a level with a golden bubble inside.
When the bubble floated right in the middle,
it meant that what we were measuring was straight.

He needed the level to fix the screen door.

That broken screen door was a wreck.

We got new hinges for it
and a hook-and-eye latch to
fasten it shut at night.

HINGES

HOOK-AND-EYE LATCH

Flora found a saw that wasn't rusty.
This one was shiny and beautiful.

**Daddy said he'd like a good, sharp saw
when he cut lumber for new kitchen shelves.**

We needed fat screws

    and long nails

        and short screws

           and skinny nails called brads

    for fixing this and that.

We picked some
from the open bins.

We found a shiny steel tape measure
that pulled out, then snapped back with a *zip*,

**and a leather carpenter's apron
where Daddy could put his tools.**

Just as we were about
to pay and leave,
Flora and I saw
a birdhouse kit.

"Can we get it? Please?"
Daddy said yes!

When we got home,
Mommy asked, "But where
are the picture hangers?"

"Uh-oh!" said Daddy.
We had forgotten them!

So off we went again,
Daddy and Flora and me.

TOOLS

←

GARDEN

Postcards

COLOR CHART

SPRAY PAINT

Back to the hardware store, filled with such interesting and handy things.

For Huang Luo Yi, aka Sullivan Wong Rockwell
—A. R.

For my parents, who always show me the fun and sense
of accomplishment in doing it yourself
—M. I.

Henry Holt and Company, LLC
Publishers since 1866
175 Fifth Avenue, New York, New York 10010
mackids.com

Henry Holt® is a registered trademark of Henry Holt and Company, LLC.
Text copyright © 2016 by Anne Rockwell
Illustrations copyright © 2016 by Melissa Iwai

Library of Congress Cataloging-in-Publication Data
Rockwell, Anne F.
Let's go to the hardware store / Anne Rockwell ; illustrated by Melissa Iwai. — First edition.
pages   cm
Summary: When the new house needs fixing up, a brother and sister accompany their father on a trip
to the hardware store to find the tools and materials needed to get the job done.
ISBN 978-0-8050-8738-3 (hardback)
[1. Hardware stores—Fiction. 2. Dwellings—Maintenance and repair—Fiction.] I. Iwai, Melissa, illustrator. II. Title.
PZ7.R5943Le 2016   [E]—dc23   2015003255

Our books may be purchased in bulk for promotional, educational, or business use.
Please contact your local bookseller or the Macmillan Corporate and Premium Sales Department
at (800) 221-7945 ext. 5442 or by e-mail at MacmillanSpecialMarkets@macmillan.com.

First Edition—2016 / Designed by Patrick Collins
Acrylics, collage, Adobe Photoshop, and Adobe Illustrator were used to create the illustrations for this book.
Printed in China by Macmillan Production Asia Ltd., Kowloon Bay, Hong Kong (vendor code 10)

1 3 5 7 9 10 8 6 4 2